A Parsnip Called Val

"Wayne has to make everyone look small," said Casper.

"He always has to be top dog," said Annie.

Dan sighed. "We've got to teach him a lesson."

"We're not going to fight him, are we?" asked Casper.

"Of course not," said Dan.

Casper looked relieved.

The idea came to Dan in a flash. "Baseball!" he cried.

More *brilliant* Young Hippo School stories:

SYLVIA GREEN

A Parsnip Called Val

Illustrated by Jacqueline East

For Stephen and Sally

Scholastic Children's Books,
Commonwealth House, 1-19 New Oxford Street,
London WC1A 1NU, UK
a division of Scholastic Ltd
London ~ New York ~ Toronto ~ Sydney ~ Auckland

Published in the UK by Scholastic Ltd, 1997

Text copyright © Sylvia Green, 1997
Illustrations copyright © Jacqueline East, 1997

ISBN 0 590 19366 X

Typeset by Backup Creative Services, Dorset
Printed by Cox & Wyman Ltd, Reading, Berks

2 4 6 8 10 9 7 5 3 1

Chapter 1

Val Parsnip

Dan stamped out of the supermarket. "The worst thing that school ever did was teach Maisie to read."

"Don't be silly," said his mother. "That's one of the main reasons she goes to school."

"But did they realize what they were doing?" Dan roughly pushed his glasses to the top of his nose. "How we would have to suffer?"

"I must admit she's making my head spin," said his mother.

All round the supermarket Maisie had been practising her reading.

"Baked Beans. Soup. Tom-a-toes." Her little high-pitched voice rang round the aisles.

Now she was reading down the till receipt. "Eggs. Ba-con."

"It'd be more use if you helped us load this stuff into the car," Dan grumbled.

"Peas," read Maisie. "Val Parsnip."

"What?"

"Val Parsnip," said Maisie. "That big parsnip with the long tail you bought, Mum. It's called Val."

"Don't be daft," said Dan. "Parsnips are vegetables. They don't have names."

Maisie wasn't listening. She was rummaging in the bag of vegetables. "You can't eat it."

Mrs Muffet took the list. "Look, Maisie," she said, pointing to it. "Val is short for value. See, the next item is Value Beans. There wasn't room on the receipt to put Value Parsnip so they shortened it to Val."

But Maisie wasn't having it. She had rescued the parsnip from the bag and was studying it. "Look, it's got eyes too."

"Vegetables often have those marks on them," her mother explained. "I bought it especially for tonight's dinner. Your dad's very fond of parsnip in his casserole."

Maisie clutched the large parsnip to her chest, her little mouth set firm.

That evening the family had casserole –
with meat, onions, carrots, and turnip.
But no parsnip. Val was asleep upstairs,
tucked neatly under the covers of
Maisie's doll's pram.

As soon as they'd finished eating, Dan
rushed out to Mission Control. It was the
garden shed really, but the space-mad
gang had put up pictures of spaceships
and aliens round the walls.

Annie arrived first and gave their secret knock. Three taps, pause, two taps, pause again and then one last tap. Casper followed close behind. The three friends were meeting to discuss the American Week they were having at school.

Annie showed them the American flag she had painted on the back of one of her mum's old tea towels. "There's the thirteen red stripes for the original thirteen states," she told them. "Then I drew fifty stars for the fifty states there are now and painted round them in blue. What do you think?"

"Great," said Dan.

The shed door opened and Maisie burst in.

"You can't come in, we're having a gang meeting," said Dan.

"I want to be in your gang," said Maisie. "So does Val."

"Who?" Casper looked past Maisie for her friend.

"Don't ask," said Dan.

"I don't mind if she stays," said Annie.

Maisie smiled. Annie was always nice to her.

"Okay with me," said Casper. "What you got there, Maisie? It looks like a—"

"That," said Dan, adjusting his glasses, "is Val. And yes, it is a parsnip."

"A parsnip called Val?" said Annie.

Val now had a ribbon tied round the little tufty bits on the top where the leaves had been cut off.

Annie took a closer look. "It's a very large parsnip," she said. "Must be twenty-five centimetres long."

Dan explained to the others what had happened.

"Oh well, looks like we've got five in the gang now," laughed Casper.

"I just hope Wayne doesn't find out we've got a parsnip as a member," Dan groaned.

Wayne was in their class at school. He was a bit of a bully.

"He's really showing off at the moment," said Casper. "Just because he's been to America and no one else has."

Annie picked up the flag. "I'll hang this up over here."

Maisie lifted the corner. "Irish Lin-en," she read.

"It doesn't matter what it says, it's the American flag," said Dan. "We're being Americans this week."

"Here, I brought some cookies," said

Casper, handing the packet round.

"Rich Tea," read Maisie. "They're biscuits."

"Biscuits are called cookies in America," Dan told her.

"And I brought some candy," said Annie.

"Wine Gums," read Maisie.

"Ignore her," Dan sighed. "Anyone got any root beer?"

Chapter 2

The Space Shuttle

The first lesson at school the next morning was baseball. Wayne was wearing a real American baseball hat with NEW YORK YANKEES on it and was showing off as usual.

"That's not a baseball bat," he said. "It's a rounders bat. I saw the real ones when I was in America."

"We haven't got a baseball bat, Wayne," said Miss Turner patiently. "But it doesn't really matter, does it? We're not playing for the League."

Everyone tittered, which made Wayne cross. "And that ball's a tennis ball," he grumbled.

"I do know that, Wayne," said their teacher. "But as we haven't got all the protective gear for you to wear I'm happier playing with a soft ball."

Dan enjoyed playing baseball but Annie was the star pupil. She loved all sports and picked up the game of baseball really quickly.

It soon became obvious that Wayne was better at talking about it than playing.

The rest of the day was spent working on a map of the United States of America. The map was divided up into the fifty states and was so big it covered two tables pushed together. They wrote in the names of the states and some of the capitals and learned a bit about each one.

Miss Turner asked them to pick a place they found interesting and do a model or a drawing about it to put on the map.

"It can be something to do with history or an activity or a famous landmark," she told them. "When you've decided come and write it on the board."

Shyam quickly chose the Statue of Liberty in New York Harbour and Michelle picked Disneyland.

Annie decided to do a drawing of the Astrodome in Houston, the first air-conditioned indoor sports stadium in the world.

"Come on, Casper," said Dan. "Before someone else gets our idea." He rushed up to claim the Kennedy Space Centre in Florida. "Model of the space shuttle," he wrote on the board.

Jina chose the Pilgrim Fathers' ship, *The Mayflower*, for Plymouth, New England.

Dan was watching Laura write "Black bears and alligators for the Okefenoke Swamp" when he caught sight of Wayne and Tommy giggling and whispering.

Wayne strode up to the board and wrote "Wayne and Tommy. Cotton Plantation in Alabama". Then they both looked over at Dan and Casper.

"They're up to something," said Dan. "And I've got a nasty feeling it involves us."

The gang met at Mission Control after dinner. Dan and Casper had collected a kitchen-roll tube and some toilet-roll centres to make the space shuttle. Annie had some paper and pens to draw her sports centre.

They worked on an upturned tea chest with their glue, paint and scissors laid out. They had plenty of pictures to copy from.

The door burst open and Maisie walked in.

"You're supposed to knock," said Dan.

"Look, Val's an American," she said, holding the large parsnip up for them to see. She had taped some pigeon feathers to the top of it. "She's a Red Indian."

"That's very good, Maisie," said Annie.

Dan peered over the top of his glasses.

"Yeah, very good. Now we're busy. So if you're going to stay, you'll have to keep quiet."

Maisie wandered to the back of the shed. Casper carefully applied some glue to the space shuttle while Dan held it.

"Grass Seed," read Maisie.

They ignored her.

"Pot-ting Com-post." She was moving round the shed. "La-a-wern. Lawen Sand."

"Lawn. It's lawn sand," said Dan. "Now for heaven's sake, Maisie, be quiet."

"I'm teaching Val to read," Maisie protested.

They were rescued then as Mrs Muffet came to get her for her bath.

"Can Val have a bath?" they heard Maisie ask as they left.

There was great excitement in the playground the next morning as children arrived carrying models and pictures.

There was an oil well for Texas and an Eskimo for Alaska. Adrian had made a very good model of the White House out of Lego. It was just a shame he had run out of white bricks and had to use some yellow.

Steve had brought some toy cars to put on Detroit and Sally had drawn some buffalo for the Great Plains. But where were Wayne and Tommy?

They found out as soon as they got inside. There they were with Miss Turner, proudly admiring a model of the space shuttle placed on the Kennedy Space Centre.

So that's what they were giggling about. Dan stormed over to them, roughly pushing his glasses to the top of his nose. "That was our project."

Miss Turner looked up, surprised.

"We wrote it on the board," he said, pointing.

Miss Turner went over to look. "No, dear, you've got mixed up. You're down for a Cotton Plantation in Alabama. Look."

Dan looked, not wanting to believe what he was seeing. "He's rubbed our names out and changed them," he hissed to Casper.

Wayne had got the better of them again.

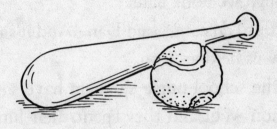

Chapter 3

Baseball

The three friends walked round the edge of the school playing-fields at breaktime. They were reluctantly collecting twigs to make a cotton plantation.

"I'm sick of Wayne," said Dan. "It's not the first time he's done something like this."

"He's really showing off about that

space shuttle," said Annie.

"Let's just make a really good cotton plantation," said Casper. "Make it look as though we don't care."

"But I *do* care," said Dan. "And it's not only us he does it to."

The school nurse let them have some cotton wool and they spent their lunch break gluing it to the twigs and painting them. They stuck all their cotton bushes into brown plasticine and the result was pretty good.

After school Dan, Annie and Casper
followed Wayne and Tommy as they
walked towards the school gates. Dan
could see his mother and Maisie waiting.
Maisie must have come out early and
they'd come to give him a lift. Maisie ran
into the playground towards him.

"Look, Dan. Look at Val," she cried.

"No. Not now," hissed Dan, waving at
her to put Val down. He tried to put
himself between her and Wayne.

But he was too late. Wayne had spotted the parsnip.

"I've made Val a skirt," said Maisie.

Dan watched Wayne's face as he stared at the parsnip with a ribbon tied round its tufty bits, two pigeon feathers sticking up and now a skirt wrapped round its long tail.

Wayne broke into a huge grin. Then he grabbed Tommy's arm and they creased up with laughter.

Dan felt himself going very red and then hot all over.

"What's the matter, Dan?" Wayne hissed. "Couldn't your parents afford a Barbie doll?" Still doubled up, Wayne and Tommy sidled off.

Dan turned on Maisie. "Why did you have to bring that here? Embarrassing me like that. It'll be all round the school tomorrow."

Maisie's face changed. Tears sprang into her usually bright blue eyes.

The gang sat gloomily in the shed, surrounded by the bits and pieces used to make their model the previous evening. Maisie didn't come out.

Dan felt dreadful. He shouldn't have shouted at his little sister like that. It wasn't her fault. If she wanted a parsnip why shouldn't she have one?

And just suppose they *had* been too poor to buy her a proper doll. It wouldn't be anything to laugh about.

"Wayne has to make everyone look small," said Casper.

"He always has to be top dog," said Annie.

Dan sighed. "We've got to teach him a lesson."

"We're not going to fight him, are we?" asked Casper.

"Of course not," said Dan.

Casper looked relieved.

The idea came to Dan in a flash. "Baseball!" he cried.

"What?"

"We'll challenge Wayne to a baseball game. He thinks he knows it all because he's been to America but he's not very good at baseball."

"No," Casper agreed. "And we all know who's the best player in the class – Annie."

"Exactly. And you're on our side, aren't you, Annie?" said Dan.

"Course I am. We'll thrash him."

"Wayne will look really silly when he loses after all the boasting he's done," said Casper.

Dan stood up and adjusted his glasses. "And Val will be our team mascot. No one will bother laughing at me if I'm not embarrassed."

"Great," laughed Annie.

When Dan suggested the baseball match to Miss Turner she thought it was a very good idea. She said it would make a good end to American Week. It was agreed to hold it the next day, Friday, after school when parents could come and watch.

The class gathered round so that the two captains, Dan and Wayne, could choose the teams.

Wayne will pick Tommy, Sharon, and a few others who hang around with him, Dan thought. I'll obviously pick Annie and Casper. Probably Shyam and Laura too. They needed nine players on each side. The rest could be reserves.

"Choose one at a time," said Miss Turner. "Wayne, you start."

Dan watched him look slowly over the class. Come on, he thought. It's obvious you're going to pick Tommy first.

"Annie," said Wayne.

Chapter 4

We're Not Quitters!

Dan walked home slowly, with his head bowed. "I never dreamed he'd choose you for his team, Annie. We haven't got a chance without you."

"We should have realized he knew that Annie was easily the best player," said Casper. "If only he hadn't picked first."

"I won't play well," said Annie. "I'll

miss the ball when I'm batting and I'll drop it when I'm fielding."

"You can't do that," said Dan. "It'll be obvious what you're doing. Everyone knows how good you are. It'll make us look even worse."

"Well I won't go. I'll pretend I'm sick," said Annie.

Dan shook his head. "That won't work, either."

"If only we had someone else who's good," said Casper. "No one else plays as well as you, Annie."

Annie suddenly stopped. "It's obvious what you do."

"What?"

"You'll have to practise."

"But we haven't got another baseball lesson," said Casper.

"No. I mean now. I'll help you." She

started to run. "Come on."

"She's right," said Dan, chasing after her. "We're not quitters!"

Casper ran after them. "We've been talking like Annie was going to win the game on her own," he puffed. "Even with her on our team we would still have to try our best."

As soon as they got to Dan's house they started practising pitching and catching.

Maisie was delighted that Val was to be the team mascot. She brought her out to watch.

After dinner, Annie brought along her rounders bat and they practised batting until their arms ached.

"You've picked it all up so quickly, Annie," said Casper.

"I always do when it's games," said Annie. "But anything like Maths and I'm hopeless."

Dan began to feel happier. Now they could at least put up a fight.

"Ah-choo! Ah-choo!" Dan awoke the next morning full of hay fever. His eyes were itching and streaming, and his nose running.

"It's probably because you spent so much time outside amongst the grass last night," said his mother.

"I thought it was better this year," Dan grumbled. "How am I going to play baseball?"

"Use your nasal spray," said his mother. "That usually helps. You'll just have to hope there isn't any long grass near where you're playing."

Dan felt a bit better by the time he got to school. The caretaker had marked out the diamond-shaped baseball pitch on the playing-field. He had secured canvas bags to the ground to mark the first, second and third bases. And somehow he had made up a home plate and a pitcher's plate.

"It looks so – so *real*," said Annie, her eyes shining.

"I think Mr McEvoy has done a wonderful job," said Miss Turner.

Even Wayne agreed with that.

They spent the morning learning about the different Native American tribes that had been the first inhabitants of America. Dan decided that when he was older he was definitely going to visit America.

During the afternoon they went over the rules for the baseball game again and picked the positions for the fielders. Miss Turner decided they would have only six innings, as the usual nine would take too long. Each team would still have six chances to bat.

At last, it was time for the actual game. Dan could feel the tension rising as they changed into their games kits. He started to sneeze again.

Wayne was watching him. "Are you ill?" he asked.

"No. It's only hay fever," Dan told him, reaching for his spray. "I'm allergic to grass pollen. But don't worry, I can still beat you."

"Ha. That'll be the day," Wayne laughed.

Outside, Miss Turner handed out red bands for Wayne's team to wear.

"We're called Wayne's Whackers," he announced.

Dan's mind whirled as he took the blue bands for his team. "Dan's Dodgers," he said quickly.

Miss Turner went to welcome the parents and brothers and sisters that had come to watch.

"You're using the wrong bat. And the pitcher's plate should be on a mound."

Everyone looked round. It was Wayne's mum who had spoken.

So that's where he gets it from, thought Dan.

"The exercise has been to teach the children the basics of one of America's favourite games," Miss Turner told her. "This is just a friendly game to finish off American Week."

Friendly? Dan and Wayne stared at each other. Both knew that this was definitely not "just a friendly game".

Chapter 5

Wayne's Whackers v. Dan's Dodgers

Wayne's Whackers were first to bat. They made their way to the batters' bench which had been placed on the edge of the field. Wayne swaggered on to the pitch to bat first. He was wearing his NEW YORK YANKEES baseball cap and he waved to the crowd, holding the bat up in a salute. A couple of his followers shouted to him and his mum cheered embarrassingly loudly. Several people looked round at her but she didn't seem to notice.

Dan took up his place as the pitcher and spotted Mum and Maisie just to the right of the batter's box. Maisie held Val up for him to see. She had made her a new blue skirt for the occasion.

Dan waved to her. He'd show everyone. At least he *hoped* he would.

Casper took his position as first baseman for the Dodgers. Bawani was second baseman, and Shyam third. Steve was the catcher, Sally was shortstop and Adrian, Jina and Laura the outfielders.

Dan nervously passed the ball from hand to hand as he looked at Wayne. He had to pitch the ball into the strike zone which was over the home plate, and between the batter's knees and armpits.

"Play," called Miss Turner.

This is it then, thought Dan, adjusting his glasses. He swung his arm back as Annie had taught him and pitched the ball to Wayne. It was a good pitch.

Wayne swung his bat and missed. Steve caught the ball behind him and threw it back to Dan.

"Strike," called Miss Turner.

"That wasn't fair, I wasn't ready," said Wayne.

He would say that, thought Dan.

"Wayne." Miss Turner looked cross.

"But I really wasn't ready. I swear," Wayne insisted. His mother stood up.

"All right, Wayne," Miss Turner sighed. "Just this once I'll allow it again. But in future make sure you're ready."

Wayne smiled sweetly at her and raised the bat over his right shoulder. "I'm ready now."

Dan pitched again and Wayne hit the ball. He dropped the bat and ran towards first base. Bawani pounced on the ball and threw it to Casper. Casper caught it and touched first base just before Wayne reached it.

Wayne was out! He looked briefly towards Miss Turner but obviously thought better of protesting again. He slunk off to join the rest of his team on the bench while the Dodgers cheered.

"Brilliant," Dan shouted, as Casper returned the ball to him. What a great start to the match.

Tommy hit the ball on his second attempt and started to run. Sally gave a shriek as it hurtled towards her. She caught it. Tommy was out too.

Sharon was next. She missed the ball three times which meant three strikes against her and she was out. With three members of the team out that was the end of the Whackers' first turn to bat.

Dan was chuffed to bits. They had managed to stop the Whackers making any runs. Things were looking good.

It was the Dodgers' turn to bat. Dan nervously adjusted his glasses as he took up his place in the batter's box. He hit the ball on his second attempt and raced towards first base. Annie was first baseman and someone threw the ball to her to put him out. He saw her hesitate. What was she going to do?

He was almost there when Annie turned and placed her foot firmly on the base.

"Out," called Miss Turner.

"Sorry, Dan," said Annie.

Dan shrugged. She'd had to do it. It would have been very obvious if she hadn't.

He watched hopefully as Sally made a good hit. But Sharon caught her out. Jina had more luck, she made it to first base. Then Steve came up to bat.

Come on, Steve, thought Dan. Give it a good whack then both you and Jina can get running. He did, but Steve was left-handed and hit the ball towards first base – where Annie was. She leapt in the air and caught it.

That was their three outs. They hadn't scored a run.

Dan was disappointed but still hopeful. The Whackers hadn't scored either – and he didn't intend to let them.

It was the second inning now and the

Whackers' turn to bat again.

Annie came up to bat. She gave the ball a tremendous hit and ran right round to third base while the outfielders chased the ball. Jonathan also made a hit and Annie ran like the wind to the home plate. She had scored a run – the first of the match.

Dan wasn't really surprised – Annie was a brilliant player. But he felt really disappointed as the Whackers cheered like mad.

Wayne's team was leading 1-0. They had to stop anyone else getting a run. The Whackers mustn't build up a bigger lead.

Jonathan made it to first base but Bawani tagged him at the second. Then Justin and Winston were both caught out.

Dan was relieved. It was the Dodgers' turn to bat again. They had to make a run.

Bawani came up to bat. She made first base and then Adrian hit the ball. Dan kept his fingers crossed as they both ran. Bawani reached second but Annie put Adrian out at first.

There was still hope for Bawani. Shyam made a hit and ran to first.

Dan held his breath as Bawani raced towards third. "Oh, no," he cried. She was tagged before she reached it. He watched anxiously as Casper came up to bat. He made a good hit but he was caught out by Jonathan.

They were out again with no runs.

It was still 1-0 and the Whackers' turn to bat again at the start of the third inning.

Dan was getting very worried as he watched Wayne swagger up to the batter's box.

Laura was pitching for the Dodgers as Miss Turner wanted several of them to have a turn. She pitched the ball way over Wayne's head and he made no attempt to hit it.

"Ball," called Miss Turner. "You were outside the strike zone, dear," she told Laura.

Laura was giggling as she pitched again. This time the ball was too low. Wayne was tut-tutting and rolling his eyes.

Her next pitch was too far to the left.

She was giggling even more now. Dan

anxiously pushed his glasses to the top of his nose as he watched. That was three balls. She was only allowed one more. She wasn't taking it seriously.

The fourth pitch went too high again.

"Ball," said Miss Turner. "Wayne is awarded a base on balls as Laura has pitched four balls outside the strike zone."

That meant Wayne was allowed to walk to the first base without even attempting to hit the ball.

Dan felt numb as Wayne swaggered to the first base, waving his fist victoriously in the air. His mother stood up and cheered.

Good grief, thought Dan. He didn't exactly do anything himself.

Laura couldn't stop giggling and she pitched four more balls – all outside the strike zone – to Tommy. He was allowed to walk to first base and even worse, Wayne walked to second. The Whackers roared.

She's making us look stupid, thought Dan. She's not even trying. "Laura," he shouted to her. "Watch what you're doing."

Her next pitch was better and Sharon hit it. Dan watched in horror as Wayne headed for the home plate. He made it. Wayne had scored a run! He'd be unbearable now. And his mother would be hoarse if she didn't stop cheering.

Chapter 6

Ah-choo!

The Whackers were put out with no more runs. To Dan's dismay the Dodgers didn't make any runs either. At the end of the third inning Wayne's Whackers were leading 2-0.

They stopped for a short break as Jina's mother had brought in some real American cola for the teams and

Sharon's father had brought some Maryland cookies.

Dan was feeling terrible. This hadn't been such a good idea after all. It was all going wrong. Instead of teaching Wayne a lesson they'd given him even more reason to show off.

The whole team seemed to have lost heart and Laura was sulking because Dan had shouted at her.

"It's only a game," she protested.

"No it's not," said Casper. "We wanted to beat Wayne to teach him a lesson."

"Why?"

"Because he's always making everyone else look small," said Dan.

"That's true," said Jina. "He made me look really silly in that play we did last term. He kept standing in front of me so the audience couldn't see me."

"But what can we do about it?" asked Laura. "It's hard to pitch the ball in the right place and it's hard to hit it."

"And Wayne's got Annie in his team," Bawani added.

"I know all that," said Dan. "But we're not that bad and you're pretty good, Bawani. We've just got to try harder."

They looked over to Wayne's team.

He was showing off, as usual. When he saw Dan looking, Wayne put his arm round Annie's shoulders as if they were best friends. "We make a great team, don't you think?" he called to Dan. "One run each so far. And that's only the beginning."

Annie quickly shrugged him off.

Dan turned away.

"I'm sorry, Dan," said Laura. "He wouldn't have got that run if I had been playing properly."

"Well, like you said, it *is* hard," said Dan. "Let's just all make a really big effort. We've got three more innings to go. We can still do it."

"Yeah, let's whack the Whackers," shouted Casper.

Maisie brought Val over to see them. Casper admired the parsnip's new blue skirt.

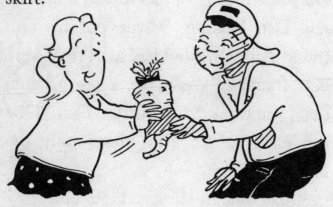

"Are you winning?" Maisie asked.

"Well, not exactly," Dan told her. He looked at her face. She was so excited. "But we will."

"Val will give you a kiss for good luck," said Maisie.

"No, I don't think—" Dan started. But he was too late, the parsnip was quickly pressed against his face.

The others laughed and Dan joined in.

Everyone was in much better spirits as they went out for the start of the fourth inning.

Sally was pitching and Dan had taken her place as shortstop. He was feeling quite hopeful again and even his hay fever wasn't giving him too much trouble.

Annie came up to bat. She hit the ball and started to run. The ball was heading towards Dan. He ran forward, hands outstretched. He caught it. He'd caught Annie out!

No one cheered louder than Annie.

Then she suddenly clapped her hand over her mouth as she remembered she wasn't supposed to be pleased.

Dan looked across to Casper and they both laughed.

Justin and then Winston were put out and Dan felt more cheerful. At least they had stopped the Whackers making any more runs.

The Dodgers were playing with a new determination. When it was their turn to bat Bawani strode on to the field. She smashed the ball into the outfield and raced right round to second base. Then

Adrian hit it and made first while Bawani made third. Shyam hit it and Bawani made it to home base.

She'd made a run! Their first. It was 2-1 now. Things were looking up and there were still another two innings to go.

It was the fifth inning now and the Whackers' turn to bat. Dan's Dodgers were fielding well, with Casper pitching. Dan thought that Annie's coaching had really paid off. Wayne looked furious as he was caught out. Tommy was out with three strikes against him.

Then disaster struck. Bawani leapt in the air and caught Sharon out but she twisted her ankle as she landed.

"Oh, no," cried Dan. "You're our best player."

Michelle was brought on as the reserve but they were all upset at losing Bawani.

It was the Dodgers' turn to bat. They tried, they really tried, but Sally, Jina, and Laura were all out. There were no more runs for the Dodgers.

Only one more inning to go. One more chance for each team.

Wayne was looking very sure of himself as he waved to the crowd. His mother cheered again.

Annie made another run. Dan watched her face as she raced towards the home plate. She really was good. She couldn't have played a bad game if she'd tried. But it spelt disaster for the Dodgers. They managed to put Jonathan, Justin and Winston out but they were now 3-1 down.

When the Dodgers came up to bat for their final inning Dan didn't feel at all hopeful. The game was rapidly slipping away from them.

Michelle was out on her way to first base, then Adrian made it all the way round to third base but was tagged by the third baseman.

Two already out. One more out and the game would be over with the pitiful score of 3-1. Dan was feeling more and more depressed. He should never have suggested this game. It was a disaster.

Shyam came up to bat. Wayne was pitching and was really showing off. He was trying to imitate the professional pitchers and was using exaggerated body movements, twisting and stretching his body before releasing the ball.

Shyam hit the ball and made it to first base. Then Casper came up to bat. On the second attempt he hit the ball to the ground and it bounced rapidly, spinning along the field. Casper ran. So did Shyam. Casper made it to second base and Shyam to third.

It was Dan's turn to bat. His heart started to beat faster as he looked at the situation. If he could just hit the ball Shyam might make it to home base. If he could only hit it hard enough then possibly Casper could make it too. They could make two runs and equal the score. That wouldn't look so bad.

He noticed Maisie edging out of the crowd towards him.

"Keep back," said Miss Turner.

Tommy was behind him as the catcher. "You're almost beat," he hissed.

Dan ignored him. He crouched low, holding the bat over his right shoulder and watched Wayne go into his pitching routine. Dan swung the bat and missed.

"Strike," called Miss Turner.

"The game's almost ours," Tommy whispered.

Wayne pitched again. Dan swung at the ball and hit it. But it went behind, into foul territory.

"Strike," called Miss Turner.

Sweat ran down Dan's face. His glasses kept sliding down his nose and he hastily pushed them back. One more strike and he would be out. The whole team would be out. They would have lost.

He saw Wayne making signs to Tommy behind him, but he had no time to wonder what they were about. This was Dan's last chance. The last chance of the match. Wayne raised the ball above his head with both hands. Dan watched him bring the ball down slowly behind him, swinging his left leg forward at the same time.

It was as though they were the only two on the baseball pitch.

Suddenly, Dan felt a puff of wind blow across his face from behind. He gasped and realized, too late, that he had breathed in a handful of grass pollen. Tommy! So that was—

His eyes and nose filled. *"Ah-choo!"*

The sneeze was so violent that his glasses shot right off. As he tried to save them the bat slipped from his sweating hands. Through his watering eyes he couldn't see where they had gone.

In the distance, he could just make out Wayne pitching the ball.

Chapter 7

Val Saves the Day

"Dan."

It was Maisie's voice, beside him.

In one movement he grabbed Val by her long tail and swung her at the ball. He hit it. An enormous hit.

"Run! Run!" Everyone was shouting.

He began to run, squinting to see where he was going. "Ah-choo," he went, but kept running towards first base.

He glanced up, to see two of the outfielders running towards the ball. He had hit a real fly-ball high into the air.

They'll catch that for sure, he thought, but he kept running.

He'd just reached first base when he saw it happen. The two outfielders collided and missed the ball.

"Run! Run!" the crowd screamed. Annie shrieked louder than anyone else.

He made second base and briefly wondered where Casper and Shyam had got to. Had they made it back to home base?

He ran on, encouraged by the crowd. He made third!

"Ah-choo." His eyes streamed. He could hardly see at all now. Where was the ball? What was happening?

"This way! Keep running." He heard Casper's voice and ran towards it.

Something whistled past his head. It had to be the ball. A shadowy figure just ahead of him caught it. They were running towards Dan. Or was it towards the base? Dan couldn't see. The fielder had only to touch him or the base and he was out.

Dan ducked to avoid the figure and at the same time saw the home plate. He threw himself sideways and forwards. His right foot slid against the home plate just ahead of the fielder.

He'd done it. They'd won! Shyam and Casper were safely back, equalizing the score, and now he'd taken it one over. They'd won 4-3!

"Wow! A home run," said Tommy, standing over him with the ball.

"Ah-choo," Dan exploded.

Everyone crowded round him and someone handed him his glasses and a large handkerchief.

He saw Wayne's mother striding across the field. "Wayne. You've let me down," she cried. "You let that boy beat you."

Wayne stood with his head bowed. "Poor Wayne," said Dan. "No wonder he always has to be the best, with a mother like that."

"I'd be so embarrassed if she was my mother," whispered Casper.

Wayne's mother marched up to Miss Turner. "That wasn't fair. You can't allow it. That boy hit the ball with a – a – *vegetable*."

"You said yourself we weren't playing with a proper bat anyway," said Miss Turner. "Dan hit the ball fair and square."

"But—"

Miss Turner faced Wayne. "And if there's any more arguing I'll want a word with you and Tommy. Don't think I didn't notice what caused Dan to start sneezing like that."

Instantly, Wayne smiled at Dan. He held his hand out to him. "Well done, Dan. The Dodgers won fair and square. It was a great game."

"Good boy," said Miss Turner.

"Well you know what they say," said Wayne. "It takes a good man to win but an even greater one to accept defeat."

Dan laughed. Trust Wayne to still try and be top dog. But he didn't blame him any more. Not now he'd met his mother.

Suddenly, he looked down and saw Val lying on the ground. Slowly, he bent to pick her up. Her skirt and ribbon were gone. Only one bent pigeon feather remained on the now battered parsnip.

Dan looked up into Maisie's face. Her bottom lip was quivering and she looked very much as if she was trying not to cry.

"Did you win?" she asked.

"Yes – er – look, Maisie, I'm sorry about Val."

"Did Val help you win?" asked Maisie.

"Yes. I couldn't have won without her," said Dan. "In fact, Val saved the day."

"Did she?" said Maisie, brightening up.

Annie put her arm round her as they walked off the field. "We'll get you another one on the way home," she said.

"Or how about a tomato called Bar?" said Dan.

"That's short for bargain," whispered Casper.

"Not necessarily," said Dan. "It could be short for Barbara."

The End